For the knights who say "NI!"

IMPRINT
A part of Macmillan Children's Publishing Group,
a division of Macmillan Publishing Group, LLC

ABOUT THIS BOOK
Artist's medium is digital, Photoshop, and Wacom Cintiq. The text was set in Caecilia LT,
and the display type is hand-drawn. The book was edited by Erin Stein and designed
by Natalie C. Sousa. The production was supervised by John Nora,
and the production editors were Christine Ma and Hayley Jozwiak.

Library of Congress Cataloging-in-Publication Data
Names: Mayer, Kirsten, author. | Horton, Laura K., illustrator.
Title: Go big or go gnome! / Kirsten Mayer ; illustrated by Laura K. Horton.
Description: First edition. | New York : Imprint, 2017. | Summary: Although
unable to grow a beard, Al the garden gnome, after discovering his talent
for barbering, wins a special award at the beard contest.
Identifiers: LCCN 2016009014 | ISBN 9781250111272 (hardback)
Subjects: CYAC: Gnomes—Fiction. | Beards—Fiction. | Barbers—Fiction. |
BISAC: JUVENILE FICTION / Humorous Stories. | JUVENILE FICTION / Social
Issues / Self-Esteem & Self-Reliance. | JUVENILE FICTION / Nature & the
Natural World / General (see also headings under Animals).
Classification: LCC PZ7.M4613 Go 2017 | DDC [E]—dc23
LC record available at https://lccn.loc.gov/2016009014

Our books may be purchased in bulk for promotional, educational,
or business use. Please contact your local bookseller or the
Macmillan Corporate and Premium Sales Department at (800) 221-7945 ext. 5442
or by e-mail at MacmillanSpecialMarkets@macmillan.com.

Imprint logo designed by Amanda Spielman

First Edition—2017

1 3 5 7 9 10 8 6 4 2

mackids.com

Do not steal this book without permission from the gnome who owns it.
Also, never pull a gnome's whiskers. Furthermore, don't steal shrubbery. Somegnome worked very hard on it.

GO BIG OR GO GNOME

Kirsten Mayer

illustrated by Laura K. Horton

{Imprint}
MAKE YOUR MARK

NEW YORK

This is Albert the Gnome.
You can call him Al.

Al lives in a hollowed-out mushroom cap
with a roof of pinecone shingles
and a front door made of
a sturdy acorn top.

Al works in a garden with other gnomes.

Melvin sweeps up sticks and stones.

Earl rakes rows of very small rocks.

Bartleby has dandelion duty, fluffing the fluff.

Cliff bathes the birds and fills the fountains.

Harold wrangles wiggly worms.

Al takes care of the shrubbery, trimming a leaf here and there to keep it tidy.

His best friend, Gnorm, sweeps up after him.

See how all these busy gnomes have imperial beards and illustrious mustaches?

All of them do—except Al.

He tries and tries,
but he can't grow a single whisker on his face.

That's too bad for Al, because the biggest event
of the year for gnomes is the B.I.G.—
the Beards International Gnome-athlon.

B.I.G.

Everygnome in the garden grooms and prunes, primps
and crimps to win trophies for Longest Beard,
Bushiest Beard, and Overall Best Beard.

Everygnome . . . except Al.

"This really gets my goatee," says Gnorm.
"It's not fair for you to be left out."

Al strokes his smooth chin thoughtfully.
"I have an idea!"

This is Englebert the Gnome,
the Grandmaster Judge of Whiskers.

It takes a lot to impress old Englebert.

The first contest is for Longest Beard.
Gnomes line up to see whose scruff is the most inchworms long.

Al steps up next, and he has a beautiful, long white beard!
It's so light and fluffy that it floats in the air.

"Well, what have we here? Did Albert finally sprout some whiskers?"
asks Englebert, chuckling.

When the old gnome leans in for a closer look, something tickles his nose.
He lets out a great big ACHOO! and dozens of tiny white butterflies flutter away.

"FALSE BEARD!" roars Englebert.

The next competition is for Bushiest Beard.
Al's beard is now a unique reddish color and very bushy.

"Did that beard just twitch?" asks the old gnome.

"Oh no, sir, I just wiggled my chin," says Al.

Suddenly, there is a chitter under Al's cap.
Englebert whisks it off and
uncovers a squirrel!

"FALSE BEARD!" he roars.

Gnorm smushes some moss onto Al's face,
but it just plops to the ground.

"It's no use," says Al. "I'm just a boring barefaced gnome. I'll never win
Longest or Bushiest or Overall Best Beard.
I'll never be a winner. Not ever."

Al goes home and trims some shrubbery to keep himself busy.

A little while later, Gnorm runs up in a panic.

"Al! Al! I need your help!
I got tree sap in my beard, and now it's stuck!" he says.
"I'll never win Best Beard tomorrow! Can you fix it?"

Al goes to work.

He snips and clips all the tree sap out of his friend's beard.

Then he trims a little more.

"There you go. I did what I could," says Al.
"It's a little . . . different."

Gnorm runs to the birdbath
to look at his reflection in the water.

His new beard looks gnome-tastic!

"Wow, Gnorm, that's some beard you have there!" says Bartleby.

"It's a real zinger!" says Cliff. "Where'd you get it?"

"Al trimmed my beard for me. Now I'll win Best Beard for sure!"
Gnorm shouts as he jumps up and down.

"Sure it's real?" asks Melvin, giving it a yank.

"Maybe I should get a beard trim from Al, too," wonders Harold.

"Last one there is a rotten acorn!" cries Earl as he takes off running.

The next morning, Al wakes up and shuffles outside.
He's shocked to see a long line of gnomes waiting in front of his house.

"Look, Al!" Gnorm says.
"Everygnome wants you to trim their beards, too!"

"I better get started. It will be a close shave to get everygnome ready in time!"

Later that day, a parade of gnomes struts through the garden,

showing off an array of amazing beards.

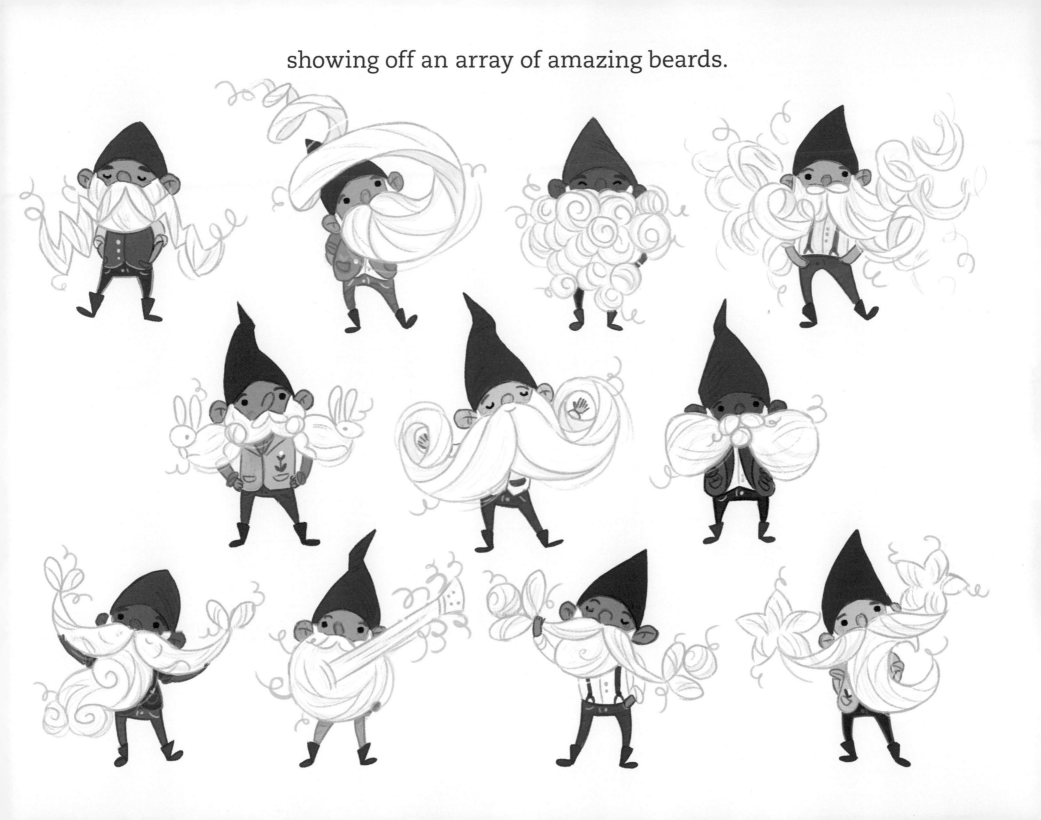

Englebert can't believe his eyes!

"Goodness grapeness!"

"Fancy feathers!"

"Whimsy and whiskers!"

"Bristles and banjos!"

Englebert claps his hands
to silence the crowd.

"Every beard here today is truly special!
I have never seen anything like it
in the history of the B.I.G.!"

"I declare the competition for Best Beard to be a thirty-way tie!
Everygnome wins!"

Englebert walks over to Al and hands him a trophy.

"Albert, you are getting a special prize. For bringing beards to
a new level and raising the handlebar for this competition,
you are the winner of the first award for Best Barber!"

Everygnome cheers as loudly as they can. Albert the Gnome is the winner!

After much celebrating, Al walks home.
He thinks about where to put his trophy.

He doesn't even notice that his light is on,
and the acorn door is slightly open . . .

"Hi, I'm Ginger."

"I was wondering,
could you give me a haircut?"